DINOSAUR

©Disney

GROLIER
B O O K S

Long ago in a forgotten time, mighty dinosaurs roamed the Earth. These dinosaurs lived off the lush, beautiful land and dwelled in harmony with each other.

One day, an enemy carnotaur,
looking for food, invaded a
peaceful colony of iguanodons.
 A mother iguanodon bravely
defended her nest of eggs.
 But one of the eggs got
taken from the nest, and it went
on a wondrous journey.

The egg had been taken away by a hungry lizard, who then dropped it into a river. The egg floated downstream and was next snatched up by a pteranodon. This huge bird carried it across a wide sea.

During the flight, the pteranodon dropped the egg above a small island. Luckily, the egg landed gently on a soft pile of leaves.

A small furry lemur named Plio found the egg in the leaves. As she did so—*CRACK*—the shell of the egg split open, and a strange-looking creature emerged.

"Dad, look!" she cried, as she cradled the infant iguanodon in her arms.

Plio's father, Yar, cautiously came near, followed by a young lemur named Zini.

"It's a cold-blooded monster from across the sea," Yar said. "Get rid of it!"

But as Plio tenderly held the happy baby, her heart opened up to him. She knew he was lost and alone. Even Yar saw that the teeny orphan needed a home.

So they decided that the baby iguanodon would become a member of their family.

The lemurs named the baby Aladar. He grew up to be big and strong.

Despite his large size, Aladar was never too big to play with his lemur friends, especially Plio's daughter, Suri.

One day, Suri and her friends shrieked with delight as they raced through the trees toward Aladar.

"Oh, no!" Aladar jokingly cried. "Attacking lemurs!"

All the lemurs jumped on Aladar and started tickling him until he couldn't take it any more.

"Okay, uncle! You got me!" laughed the ticklish dinosaur. "Come on, pick on someone your own size."

Plio interrupted their game.

"All right, guys, break it up," she said. "Remember the courtship ceremony? You're going to miss all that smooching."

The courtship ceremony was a yearly ritual when the young lemurs chose their mates.

"Go find Zini," Plio said, smiling at Aladar. "He's rehearsing pick-up lines somewhere."

Aladar found Zini near the beach, rehearsing his lines. Zini was confident he could find a mate.
    But when he arrived at the Ritual Tree for the ceremony, he got tangled in the vines. By the end of the ceremony, he was the only lemur without a mate.

Aladar knew how Zini felt. As the only iguanodon on the small island, Aladar wondered whether he himself would ever find a mate.

"Don't worry, Zini," Aladar said, cheering Zini up. "You always have next year."

Suddenly, a bright light flashed through the night sky. All the lemurs looked up in amazement.

Across the sea, a giant comet fell to the Earth. The power of this comet hitting the Earth caused a huge wave of fire. It was heading straight for the island.

"Aladar!" Plio screamed. "Where's Suri?" Plio knew something was terribly wrong.

Aladar found Suri, and he placed her and Plio on his back. Then Yar and Zini jumped on. With his family together, Aladar ran to escape the hot flames which were close behind him.

"Run, Aladar, run!" shouted Plio.

With the flames at his tail, Aladar jumped into the sea and carried everyone to safety on the Mainland.

Sadly, Lemur Island was destroyed.

So Aladar and his family started looking for a new home.

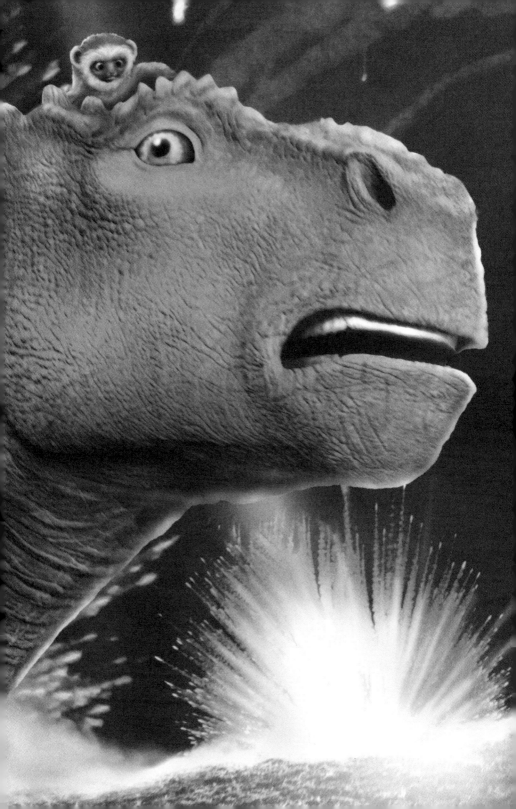

It was a hard journey. There was no food or water. But the brave group continued full of hope.

Suddenly, the ground began to shake. A huge dust storm approached them. Before they knew it, the group was surrounded by a herd of dinosaurs!

"Stay out of my way!" roared Kron, the leader of the Herd, as he marched past them.

"You heard Kron! Move it!" added Kron's lieutenant Bruton.

Aladar and the others were amazed.

"Look at all the Aladars!" Suri cried.

   After the Herd had passed quickly, a small
group of dinosaurs slowly followed along—
Baylene, Eema, and Url.
   "My name is Aladar," the iguanodon greeted
them. "This is my family."

Aladar learned from them that the Herd was on its way to a place called the Nesting Grounds.

"It is the most beautiful place there is, child." Eema explained. "It's where the Herd goes to have their babies."

Because of the comet, the journey was more difficult. And Kron was moving the Herd faster.

"We can hardly keep up," moaned Baylene.

Aladar wanted to help his new friends. So he ran ahead to speak to Kron.

Aladar quickly explained that Eema and Baylene were having a hard time keeping up with the Herd.

"So, you know, Kron," Aladar said, "maybe you can slow it down a bit?"

But Kron didn't seem to care. He believed that only the strongest should survive.

After he stormed off, Kron's sister, Neera, walked up to Aladar.

"Don't worry," she said, smiling. "That's how my brother treats newcomers—no matter how charming they are."

Aladar watched Neera as she walked away. He wondered if she had smiled at him.

The next morning, the Herd needed to reach a distant lake. But first they had to cross a large desert.

Kron told Bruton to instruct the newcomers.

"Listen up," Bruton yelled to the Herd. "If a predator catches you, you are on your own."

Eventually, the Herd arrived at the lake. But there wasn't any water in it!

Eema was ready to cry. "There has always been water here before," she moaned.

Kron realized that the explosion from the comet must have dried up the lake. So he ordered the Herd to keep moving.

But Eema was exhausted. She couldn't go on.

"Oh, Eema, please," begged Baylene. "The Herd won't wait. We'll be left behind."

Baylene stepped forward. As she did, her foot made a *squishing* sound.

Her enormous brachiosaurus foot had sunk so deep in the dirt that it had hit water.

Aladar turned and called out to the rest of the Herd. "Water! Come on!"

Later, Aladar told Neera that the Herd should be kinder to its weaker members.

"Everyone counts," Aladar explained. "If we all look out for each other, we all stand a better chance of getting to your Nesting Grounds."

Neera was surprised to hear Aladar speak so strongly. Never before had she heard such compassion.

Meanwhile, Kron watched Neera and Aladar from a nearby hill. Seeing his sister and Aladar together made him angry.

Suddenly, a voice cried out in pain. "Kron!"

Kron turned to see Bruton badly hurt. When Kron asked Bruton who had hurt him, Bruton gasped, "The carnotaurs!"

"They never come this far north," Kron said.

"The comet must have driven them out!" said Bruton.

They had to escape from their predators. Kron ordered the Herd to move out quickly.

Aladar wanted to be close to Neera at the front. But he had a responsibility to his friends at the back.

"Come on, you guys," Aladar urged. "We're going to get left behind!"

Aladar and the others could not keep up.

A thunderstorm moved in. As lightning flashed
and thunder roared, the wayward group got lost.

Then a shadowy figure appeared in the distance.
Was it an enemy carnotaur?

"Oh, it's Bruton," cried Eema.

Bruton looked badly hurt. Aladar offered to help him. But Bruton refused.

Just then, a flash of lightning lit up the sky. Aladar saw that Eema's pet Url had discovered the entrance to some caves.

"If you change your mind," Aladar said to Bruton, "we'll be in those caves."

Soon, Bruton did change his mind. He followed the others into the cave.

Inside the cave, Plio nursed Bruton's wounds. Bruton noticed that Aladar was encouraging the others.

"Why is he doing this, pushing them on with false hope?" Bruton asked Plio.

Plio explained, "It is hope that has gotten us this far."

Later that night, as everyone slept peacefully, the carnotaurs found the cave.

"I'll hold them off," Bruton yelled to Aladar. "Save yourself."

Bruton bravely held back the terrible carnotaurs. Aladar led the others deep into the cave.

To beat the carnotaurs, Bruton knocked down a pillar. But the pillar fell on Bruton.

The carnotaurs were beaten. But the cave was closed. Aladar and the others went deeper into the cave, desperately searching for an exit.

"Hold on a minute!" Zini said, sniffing the air. "Do you smell that?"

"Yeah!" answered Suri. It was fresh air.

They soon found a hole in the rocks. A ray of sunlight shone through.

"Everybody, stand back!" Aladar shouted, bashing into the rock wall. But a small landslide blocked out the ray of light from the outside.

Losing hope, Aladar said, "We're not meant to survive."

"Shame on you," Baylene scolded him. "You allowed an old fool like me to believe I was needed. And do you know what? You were right!"

With their last ounce of strength, together everyone rammed the rock wall until—*CRASH*—they broke through! And there lay the Nesting Grounds!

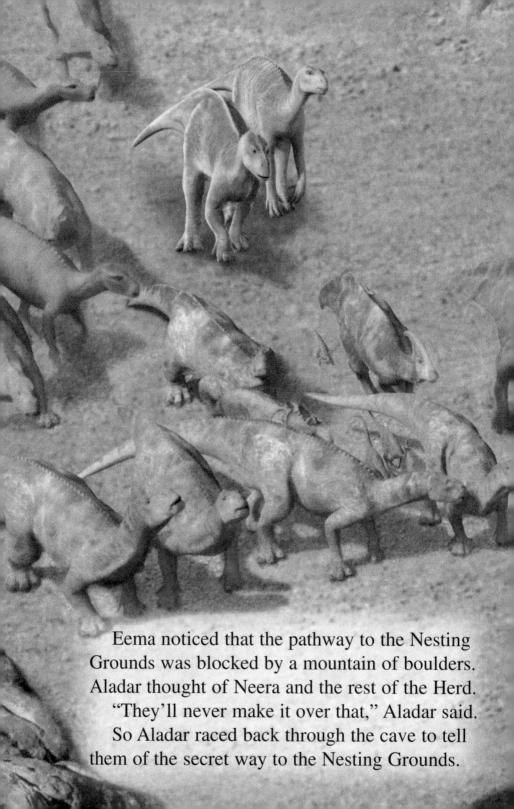

Eema noticed that the pathway to the Nesting
Grounds was blocked by a mountain of boulders.
Aladar thought of Neera and the rest of the Herd.
"They'll never make it over that," Aladar said.
So Aladar raced back through the cave to tell
them of the secret way to the Nesting Grounds.

Aladar found Kron trying to make the Herd go up the dangerous landslide that led to the Nesting Grounds.

"Stop!" Aladar cried out. "I've been to the valley. There's a safer way."

Neera encouraged her brother to listen to Aladar. But Kron was furious. Aladar was challenging his leadership. Kron rammed into Aladar and knocked him to the ground.

Suddenly, a mighty sound thundered out—
ROAR! It was a carnotaur! The Herd panicked
and began to run.

"No, don't move," Aladar told them. "If we
scatter, the carnotaur will pick us off one by
one. Stand together!"

The Herd joined Aladar. Side by side, they
bravely stood up to the carnotaur.

But suddenly, the carnotaur saw one member who stood alone—Kron.

The carnotaur charged Kron. Aladar and Neera tried to help him, but they were too late. Kron fell to the ground.

With strength, courage, and Neera's help, Aladar defeated the carnotaur. The Herd cheered wildly.

Then Aladar led everyone peacefully to the Nesting Grounds.

With Neera by his side, Aladar said, proudly, "Welcome home."

Weeks later, they gathered together to see a joyful event. A tiny egg cracked open. A beautiful iguanodon baby was born.

"He looks just like me," Aladar announced.

"Meet your dad," Neera said, smiling at her newborn. "He's not as crazy as he looks." Everyone laughed.

At long last, the lemurs and Aladar had found a wonderful new home.

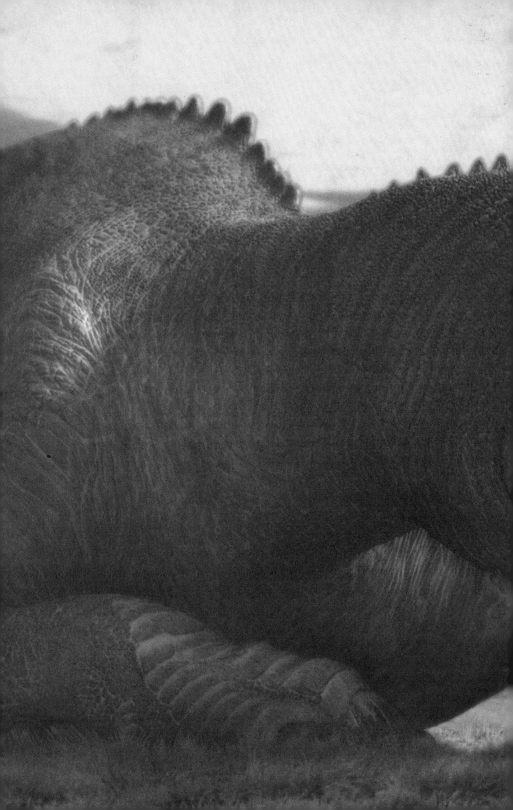